nickelodeon

PAW PATROL

DINOSAUR RESCUE!

Adapted by Hollis James

Based on the teleplay "The Pups and the Big Rumble" by David Rosenberg

Illustrated by MJ Illustrations

A Random House PICTUREBACK® Book

Random House 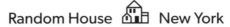 New York

rhcbooks.com

ISBN 978-0-593-18036-5

Printed in the United States of America

10 9 8 7 6 5 4 3

It was a beautiful day in Adventure Bay, and the pups were playing tug-of-war.

"Good game!" said Ryder when they were finished. "Way to tug, pups!"

Just then, Ryder's PupPad rang. He was getting a call from his pup friend Rex, who lived in Dino Land.

"Hi, Rex," said Ryder. "Is everything all right?"

"Not really, Ryder," said Rex. "There's a volcano here that looks like it's going to erupt. And a bunch of dinosaurs are right near it."

Ryder knew he and the pups had to help. "We're on our way," he said. "No dinosaur is too big, no pup is too small. PAW Patrol—to the Dino Patroller!"

With Robo Dog at the wheel, the Dino Patroller raced into a secret tunnel, splashed through a waterfall, and soon arrived in Dino Land, where Rex was waiting for them.

"Hey, Rex!" said Marshall, exiting the truck. "Good to see you!"

"You too!" replied Rex. "But we've got to hurry to save our dino friends!"

All the pups headed straight to the Dino Lookout.

"For this mission, I'll need Chase," said Ryder. "You'll have to use your siren and megaphone to get the dinosaurs' attention. Lead them to the clearing, where the lava can't reach them."

"Chase is on the case!" said Chase.

"And, Rex, I need you to use your big wheels to help Chase herd the dinos," said Ryder, "and your ability to speak Dino to tell them where they need to go."

"Let's dino-*do* it!" said Rex.

"All right," said Ryder. "PAW Patrol is on the roll!"

They quickly reached the foot of the volcano, where the dinosaurs were grazing.

"Dinos, you need to get out of here!" Chase announced through his megaphone.

But the dinosaurs didn't move.

Rex began speaking Dino to the creatures. He grunted, growled, and roared, then shouted, "Time to go! The volcano's going to blow! Hot lava!"

The dinos understood and ran to safety with Rex.

As the big dinosaurs thundered through the jungle, a baby triceratops stopped to chew on a stick. A little velociraptor tried to chomp on the same stick.

Suddenly, a protective mama triceratops bumped the raptor away from her child.

The scared little raptor rolled onto a ledge on the side of the volcano.
"I don't think he can get down," said Rex.
"You're right," said Ryder. "And he may be in the path of the lava.
I'll call Skye."

Skye sped to save the velociraptor. "Hold still and I'll get you," she said to the dinosaur.

Just as she lowered her harness, the volcano rumbled—and the little raptor slipped off the ledge! Skye immediately swooped down and caught him!

"Ryder, look what that little bit of lava did to the grass," said Chase.
"Hmm . . . this eruption could burn the whole grazing area," said Ryder.
"That's not good," said Rex. "This is the dinos' favorite place to eat!"
"I'll call in more help," said Ryder. "Rubble! Marshall!"

"Rubble, dig a trench so the lava will flow away from the grassland and into that canyon," said Ryder.

"One trench coming up!" said Rubble.

"Marshall," said Ryder, "whenever you see lava drop onto the grass, cool it down with water before it starts to burn."

As Rubble went to work digging, Marshall activated his water cannons. The jets of water quickly cooled the fiery lava, turning it into steaming rock.

Ryder helped a baby stegosaurus get into the back of Chase's truck as the other dinosaurs marched across a bridge to safety.

Suddenly, the volcano thundered fiercely. The ground shook and trees fell, blocking the bridge.

Ryder called for Rocky and Zuma, and they raced to the scene.
"Let's clear away those trees," he told them.

Rocky used the claws on his truck to lift the fallen trees out of the
way. Zuma snagged the logs with his truck's hook and hauled them off.

"Great work, pups!" Ryder cheered.

The dinosaurs had gotten across the bridge just in time—more and more lava was spilling from the volcano.

"Rubble!" Ryder yelled. "We have to get out of here!"

But Rubble wasn't done with the trench. He lifted one last scoop of dirt. . . .

"That's it!" Rubble exclaimed. Then he zoomed away with Marshall and Ryder.

The lava flowed through the trench and down into a canyon. The dinosaurs' grazing land was saved!

Just then, there was a loud **BOOM, BOOM, BOOM!**

"That volcano just won't stop," Ryder declared as he called Skye. "Check the grazing area one more time," he told her.

"That's not the volcano," Skye reported. "It's a T. rex in trouble! He's stuck near the lava!"

The Dino Patroller raced to save the T. rex.

Rex bravely raised his chair until he was face to face with the giant creature. Speaking Dino, he promised the T. rex they could help him if he just stepped onto the platform on the side of the truck.

The T. rex carefully stepped on, and the big truck roared away.

The Dino Patroller went faster and faster. But there was a river of lava in the way!

"Robo Dog," said Ryder, "use those rocks like a launching ramp!"

The vehicle hit the boulders and flew into the air. It zoomed over the lava.

The Dino Patroller landed safely with a thump. The grateful T. rex leaped off the platform and raced happily into the jungle.

The dinosaurs were safe! As Ryder and the pups left the Dino Patroller ramp, the little stegosaurus began grunting at them.

"He's saying thanks," Rex said.

"You're welcome," said Ryder. "Whenever you need to move a bunch of dinosaurs, just yelp for help!"